WEST OF DARKNESS

WEST OF DARKNESS

Emily Carr: a self-portrait

by

John Barton

Porcepic Books
an imprint of

Beach Holme Publishing
Vancouver

This book is published by Beach Holme Publishing, #226—2040
West 12th Ave., Vancouver, BC, V6J 2G2. This is a Porcepic Book.

We acknowledge the financial support
of the Canada Council for the Arts, the
Government of Canada through the
Book Publishing Industry Development
Program (BPIDP) and the assistance of
the Province of British Columbia
through the British Columbia Arts
Council for our publishing activities
and program.

The Canada Council Le Conseil des Arts
for the Arts du Canada
since 1957 depuis 1957

Editor: Joy Gugeler
Production and Text Design: Teresa Bubela
Author photograph: Mark Webster
Cover image: Emily Carr, *Edge of the Forest*, 1935; oil on paper,
86.7 x 58.4 cm, The McMichael Canadian Collection. Used with
permission.

Canadian Cataloguing in Publication Data

Barton, John, 1957-
  West of darkness

  Poems.
  ISBN 0-88878-402-3

  1. Carr, Emily, 1871-1945--Poetry.   I. Title.
PS8553.A78W4 1999   C811'.54   C99-910883-2
PR9199.3.B3753W4 1999

for Mum, Robin and Lala (who is Emily in spirit),
and in memory of Anne Szumigalski

Darest thou now O soul,
Walk out with me toward the unknown region,
Where neither ground is for the feet nor any path to follow?

—Walt Whitman

TABLE OF CONTENTS

*Italicized titles are interpretations of paintings of the same name.

IV

INVOCATION

Tell my story.
Voices catch in my throat.
Tell me stories I cannot
remember, what is
swallowed by forest.

You are raven. You are lonely.
Create totems. Extend
wings that grasp the breadth of silence,
that spread over landscape—
town, sea, forest—
at peace they should curl
like waves on your breast.

You are island.
The skin of your voice casts
spells, fleshes out the journey
the mind takes through hell.
Drop fictions. Express
what the dead cannot
breathe into life.

You are the voice I remember
dying—a still moment
the wind extends through
forest, the needles
notes to a chant that envelops
me, a chrysalid, your throat.

I am the voice in the wilderness
too silent for our country to hear.
Breathe new life into art.
Mine, an earlier story,
gives yours a new syntax.

FOREWORD

by Kate Braid

I first saw Emily Carr's paintings in the Vancouver Art Gallery shortly after I moved to British Columbia in 1970. I found them dark, depressing, indecipherable. Two years later, after living in the bush on a small, rural B.C. island, cutting firewood and working every day with wood as a construction worker, I saw her paintings again and this time I was struck by her profound understanding of trees. I was hooked.

Her journal, *Hundreds and Thousands*, published posthumously, became a powerful inspiration to me as a carpenter trying to deal, as Emily did, with being a woman in what was still a man's world. I began writing poems in response to her paintings and eventually published them. Only in two poems did I dare speak in Emily's voice for, I thought, here was a woman who clearly had her own voice: lively, original and humorous.

A few years later I had the opportunity to cross the Georgia Straight from Vancouver to visit Emily's childhood home, now a public museum in Victoria, B.C. On a shelf in the reception area I found John Barton's *West of Darkness*. I was thrilled to find another poet who had been so moved by Emily Carr he had written about her life and work. Yet how could he speak in this remarkable woman's already vivid voice, inhabit her very persona, successfully?

But John Barton does succeed. Lightly, respectfully, beautifully, he has dared to take on the voice of this fearsome, and fierce, speaker of her own truths convincingly. As I read, standing in that small, dark corridor, I forgot his words were not Emily's and lost myself in another voice, a witness to her wonder and courage. Perhaps my greatest delight was to listen to Emily (through John) dare to muse

3

on those issues which, as a very private woman of her time, she hadn't dared to speak of in her own books: her painful experience studying art in England, criticized as a dowdy colonial (*My dear Mrs. R, I'd say, touching her prayer book or quickly sugaring her cup, I didn't come to London to find myself a husband. I came hoping to paint.* "Life Class (I)"); feelings of ostrasization from the 'society girls' whose *wasp waists would have snapped if they ever dared to draw breath* "Life Class (IV)"; her love of forest and totem poles in the middle of the sometimes terrifying dark, (*Cezanne began/with light./I began in darkness* "Return from the East"); and finally her rare love for Carol Pearson, a child Emily had tried to adopt (*My whole life I had extinguished /much for art. Chasing after you I found myself/playing tag through the lightly falling dark* "Mothering Sunday: A Letter to Carol Pearson").

Barton also explores Emily's mixed feelings for her father (*Father thought himself God* "Portents"), their conversation about the facts of life (*I tried to run away,/Mister Ira, but Father/grabbed at my frock./ It ripped in his hand./'You haven't heard it all,/my dear girl,' he said* "Haro Strait"), her mournful rejection of a suitor, Mayo Padden (*my art bears not love, only greed* "East Anglia Sanitorium, 1093: A Recurring Dream") and her own death (*now darkness/draws// strength/from my eyes.//Locked in its ebb//I settle* "The Clearing").

As I read these poems on the ferry ride home, a second question occurred to me. How could a *man* take on this unique character and get away with it? John poses the same question to Emily herself when he wonders in "My Emily Carr" how she might have perceived him, not only as a man, but a gay man. He considers the possibility that Emily was his 'drag' persona, his female self. A straight man might say 'muse.' He worries she would dislike this identity but perhaps, contrarily, she would have embraced it in the same way she embraced native peoples and all those who—like herself—had been pushed aside or denigrated. Perhaps this is the very sensibility that allowed him to enter her world and take on her voice.

An astonishing number of artists continue to be inspired by the work —and life—of Emily Carr. Since finding John's book, I have found others, including a poetry book, *Emily*, published by Florence McNeil in 1975. A recent exhibit at the Vancouver Art Gallery (home of one of the world's largest Carr collections) lists several works of poetry inspired by Carr. In addition to Barton's, McNeil's and two of my own (*To This Cedar Fountain* and *Inward to the Bones: Georgia O'Keeffe's Journey with Emily Carr)*, there are: *Twelve Poems for Emily Carr* by John Weier; *For Emily Carr and Hagar* by Pam O'Rourke; and *Emily Carr's Forest* by Mary Lou Patterson. There are also three musical productions: Jean Coulthard's *D'sonoqua's Song, Canada Mosaic Suite*; Harry Freedman's *Klee Wyck*; and Veda Hille's *Here is a picture (Songs for E Carr)*. There are five plays: Joy Coghill's *Song of this Place*; Don Harron and Norman Campbell's *The Wonder of It All*; Jovette Marchessault's *The Magnificent Voyage of Emily Carr* and her radio play, *A Shaman's Voyage*; and Herman Voaden's *Emily Carr: A Stage Biography with Pictures*. Children's fiction inspired by Carr includes *Emily Carr's Woo* by Constance Horne and *Under Emily's Sky* by Ann Alma. There are also several interesting memoirs of Carr including *Emily Carr As I Knew Her*, by Carol Pearson, the almost-adopted daughter who called Emily 'mum'.

And still there are others. There are four films: Hugh Beard's *A Woman of All Sorts*; Grant Crabtree's *Klee Wyck*; and Nancy Ryley's *Growing Pains* and *Little Old Lady on the Edge of Nowhere*. There are four dances: *Passage* by Karen Jamieson Dance Company; *The Movement in Carr* by plan B; *Klee Wyck: A Ballet for Emily Carr* by Anna Wyman and Ann Mortifee; and *The Brutal Telling* by Mascall Dance and Veda Hille. Academic works include biographies by Doris Shadbolt, Maria Tippett, Paula Blanchard and Robin Laurence and analyses of her work by Shadbolt, Anne Newlands, Stephanie Walker and others. An international tour is now being planned in 2000 for the combined works of Emily Carr, Georgia O'Keeffe and Frieda Kahlo.

The above bibliography attests to Emily Carr's resilience and to her similarity to another artist figure, Virginia Woolf's *Orlando*, for Carr too refuses to die, appearing instead in ever new incarnations.

Artists, academics, old and young, all stand respectfully before her dark, turbulent canvases attracted not only by her work but by her person, a woman who shines, paradoxically, as a bright light through the glorious darkness of her works.

Emily would have gloried in such a paradox, as she did in defying the status quo. Born in 1871 in Victoria, Emily Carr was contrary, eccentric, pig-headed, sour and prickly. While oblivious to the name calling, she did develop a reputation for eccentricity. Good Victorians crossed the street to avoid association with the strange woman in her home-made, baggy gowns and hair nets, pushing a small menagerie of dogs, rat, birds and a monkey in a baby's pram. Carr was lonely but cared not a whit for what anyone thought (*a paste solitaire in Victoria's/ steel-claw setting* "Portents").

In 1912 she travelled, alone save for her pets, through coastal and central northern B.C. via freighters, fish boats and local native canoes in order to paint in careful detail the totem poles that were rapidly being destroyed by souvenir hunters and zealous Christians purging 'pagan' idols. The trips were not easy: *I am never certain of the boatman's return/....he fears what I disturb* "Blunden Harbour." Left alone in B.C. wilderness, she must have felt something more than awe or even fear: *there is an absence of red//...behind me three totems lurch...I cannot remember where I was born...I have pillaged graves for weapons/stripped brittle rags off corpses//I hunt the darkness for warmth//the raven visits me.* Leaving with her precious sketches, she reflects on the world that has left its own mark on her: *the totem nearest me/raises his arm//fist clenched//the water reddens.*

Through her wandering, she was courted by William 'Mayo' Padden, the young purser on the Ucluelet steamer whom she'd probably met on an earlier voyage north with her sister (not a painting trip). Padden followed Emily for 6000 miles and fifteen years before he finally took 'no' for an answer to his offer of marriage: *Mayo, when we met again in London, you were/a stern bit of Canada stiff on the platform/....You followed me here. My answer was firm* "East Anglia Sanitorium, 1903: A Recurring Dream." In her journal, *Hundreds and Thousands*, she claims she "did it in self-defense because it was killing me, sapping the life from me." But it was this same steely focus, this commitment to her art, that kept her painting during the many years she was resolutely ignored.

Few white people saw the value of Carr's totem pole paintings and they were further offended by their bright colours, adopted during her art studies in France. When the B.C. government refused to buy the collection, she used her small inheritance to build the 'House of All Sorts' at 646 Simcoe Street in Victoria, as a means to support herself. Soon after, World War I began and business plummeted. When needed, her studio became a room for guests and on occasion she lived in a shed in her backyard in order to rent one more suite. She despised being a land lady; when tenants angered her, she was known to turn off their water and heat and retreat to her room. To supplement her tiny income she raised dogs, made rugs and sold clay pots. Preoccupied with making a bare living, she found little time or encouragement for painting. When she did, she sometimes resorted to brown paper and house paints, unable to afford artist's supplies.

Emily Carr's life changed dramatically when Eric Brown, Director of the National Gallery of Canada, asked to include several of her works in a 1927 show titled *Canadian West Coast Art, Native and Modern*. When he provided Carr with a train ticket for the opening, she stopped in Toronto to meet the members of the Group of Seven. The rest, as they say, is history. That night her journal records the following passage: "Something has spoken to the very soul of me, wonderful, mighty, not of this world.... I have never felt anything like the power of those canvases. They seem to have called to me from some other world, sort of an answer to a great longing."

Lawren Harris particularly impressed her and she was deeply moved when he told her, "You are one of us." Exhilarated by his on-going support and friendship, she returned to Victoria at the age of fifty-six to begin the most productive period of her life. Canvases, including many of her most famous—*Big Raven, Blunden Harbour, Indian Church* (originally bought by Lawren Harris), *Above the Gravel Pit, Scorned as Timber, Beloved of the Sky*, and *Forest, British Columbia*, poured from her reclaimed studio. John Barton writes about these works and the shift they mark in style and content. Thematically she moves from native to forest themes: *the forest like myself a fragment/of God, once unnamed,/now a leviathan suddenly gentle,//suddenly waking* "Forest, British Columbia" and slowly her paintings begin to be more widely exhibited, to sell, and she leaves the boarding house behind.

In 1937 she suffered the first of three heart attacks and in 1940 moved in with her sister Alice. Although she had been writing stories for years before her heart attack, it was illness that turned her into a serious writer. Her first book, *Klee Wyck*, became a national bestseller and won a Governor General's award in 1941: *So this is immortality/ ...tea cakes and roses in December./Today I turned seventy and Klee Wyck,/after a long and difficult birth,/is spanking fresh from Oxford University Press./A few weeks old and already/she can kick up a fuss* "A Kiss for Canada". Two more books, *The Book of Small* (1942) and *The House of All Sorts* (1944) were published before she died in a nursing home near her family property in Victoria on March 2, 1945. Her remaining books—*Growing Pains, Pause: A Sketch Book, The Heart of a Peacock* and *Hundreds and Thousands: The Journals of Emily Carr*—were published after her death.

Emily Carr's life is an inspiring story of a woman who answered the call of art, who persevered and produced fresh, breathless canvases and books that continue to inspire. At the age of sixty-nine she wrote, "I don't suppose we know from moment to moment what trivial happening is going to develop into something big or is just going to snuff right out. Maybe it is a sentence in a book or a statement by someone on the radio, or a true start, like a flight or a flower or a bird, the alive in us being caught up by the alive in the universe."

Always humble, she went on to say, "When proud feelings come I step up over them to the realm of work, to the thing I want, the liveness of the thing itself." Thank you, John Barton, for voicing for all of us, in a lip sync that never falters, this same humility, high spirit and reverence for the living pleasures of forest. Thank you for capturing her devotion to her beloved West in all its darkness—and its light. And as always, thank you Emily.

I

After a fifteen-year hiatus from serious work and years of feeling rejected, Emily is discovered by the National Gallery. A group of her paintings becomes the centrepiece of a Gallery exhibition of West Coast art. East for the opening, she meets the Group of Seven. Reinspired by their vision of Canada, she returns home to Victoria. She is fifty-six years old.

You come into the world alone and
you go out of the world alone yet
you are more alone while living.

Return From The East

Where to start? Cezanne began
with light.
I began in darkness.

I was born to it,
into shadows I never took to heart
when Small,
                  but shadows
I came to know
growing into womanhood.

This darkness has made my heart
an anchor, heavy,
uneasily swayed.
I have no use for history
or the simple knowledge of day-to-day—
what-to-wear, what-to-say.
Such illuminations are falling stars,
brief and small,
foolish to wish upon.

My sisters say I am errant
as the wind, prone
to goals not worth their salt
and cigarettes, foul language
and stubbornness,
partial to what need never know
the shaping of a human heart.
After years of flouting
their every wish
I thought I had sunk into the dark
light of assent.

I grew up west of Paris, west of London,
west of New York,
in a land west of the vast emptiness
those seven men chose
to mould from darkness
the moment they stepped
from rusting shackles of light
brought from Europe
a century before.
Light made ridiculous
by the dazzlements of Van Gogh
and Renoir.
                    (These men
are but names
accidentally seeded in my mind
by the few books I've read,
by my two trips across the Atlantic
in search of art.)

It scarcely matters now.
I live in a west of darkness
made thicker by wet coastal
forests.
                    A west whose only light
has been the setting
of a way of seeing long
dead in Europe.

Walking along the Dallas cliffs,
barely aware of the rose
crêpe-de-chine light my fellows
let dredge the ocean,
I am lost in all
I have seen and heard
down east.
              Mr. Harris said
the day before I boarded my train
at Union Station: *You are one
of us, Emily,
the Group likes your work.
What it lacks in skill,
it has in heart.*

His words carried me over
the long curved back of Lake Superior,
across the prairies,
straddled the thrill of mountains.
Here on these cliffs,
my first day home,
I can just see the first stars
steady themselves
in the eastern sky.

Christmas 1927

LIFE CLASS (I)

Klee Wyck, Mrs. Redden would fret, shaking her old, well chapeaued head all the way down the great nave of Westminster Abbey or peering over her blind of newspapers at me when we would tea later at Abingdon Court. *The way you dress!* (how she'd swoon at the sight of these loose smocks I girth myself in now), *your lovely pale neck lost in a fuss of stiff lace. And the dreadful twill skirts that crossed the Atlantic with you, crikey, make me think Canada the dowager and England the precocious young miss.*

My dear Mrs. R., I'd say, touching her prayer book or quickly sugaring her cup, *I didn't come to London to find myself a husband. I came hoping to paint.*

AUTUMN IN FRANCE

My eyes shrink from this canvas,
my attempt at light.
Was I blind

to what I saw then?
free of the dreadful weight
of Paris rudeness
and dear sister Alice,
a good companion,
but fond of prattle
and good hotels.

I was at my ease to paint,
then rest,
then paint again.

Every day I would climb
the same ravine at dawn,
sketch peasants, scythes in hand,
who lived, worked, died,
a few miles' walk
from where their mothers
bore them in stone huts,
the same two rooms where their wives
sat now on rough oak chairs.
I would sketch them knitting
on sun-drenched porches,
their children so still at my elbow
I could hear my chalk shriek
like a jay giddy with heat.

I remember when I began this canvas.
It was noon.
I had climbed midway up
a steep rise,
then sat down, washed out
by the Breton sun.
                     My eyes suddenly
were trained like a prism
on the sky.
Light broke over the hills,

settling in long wind-
swept curves.
              I saw saffron
trees poke through
a mist of green.
Fields of flax, in their final
blue flower,
unfurled in bolts of mustard light.
The hills were rainbows
melting into the stunned
azure sea. Thatched roofs
wove together in flames
so vermilion my blood
runs slow to look at them now.

The next summer I found
lodgepoles and totems
up to their ears in salal,
near Alert Bay,
in Skidegate, by the Skeena;
untold histories carved
into the tranquil stares
of animals piled to their summits.

Where I would have seen darkness
a year earlier, seen only
time's talismanic decay,
I felt the wind-shined poles
stand apart from the forest,
take on in the sun
the soft mauves of mists
over Georgia Strait.
My guide's canoe cut through
into coves no man
had entered for what seemed
thousands of years.
Curled beside a beach fire,
unable to decide if I was
the first woman
or the last,
I'd watch the pole-figures
give themselves to the night.
The next morning I'd always
sketch them quickly,
like a midwife, afraid
they would vanish forever.

Fifteen years have scurried past.
Hill-House has taxed my patience,
what with bills to pay,
tenants changing.
If I string a few minutes
together and paint,
some ass taps on my door.
Miss Carr, hot water's gone.
My thoughts stick like mice
paralyzed with fear in corners
or scamper clean off,
never come back.

QUEEN CHARLOTTE ISLANDS TOTEM

Mauves I remembered faded

with so much tact the long years through,
like the sun,
these two dead eyes left
open by fingers of an unseeing hand.

The weathered poles I came to
paint should not be
this, should not be this
slow collapse into ungodliness,

so painful, primal—
termites picking clean the beaver's
fragile teeth.

Vanquished

Nature rebels: burial
poles lean into
the forest as it somersaults

across the flood plains' back,
foams up against the mountain's breast.
No one is left to stand

the totems erect.
I save what I can. Yet so small
am I, a bewildered child

measuring time with a leaky
spoon, I am swept
into the moment's vengeance

in spite of myself. I clutch
what little I have
in this growing

dark and spin like a bloated
stump of cedar sent
stumbling up the beach. I can't see

lost as I am in waves.
Whatever was buried in my heart
is heartlessly churned up

like shells of the long dead.
Memory abandons me.
The totems lean

stubbornly every which way.
The clouds above
puff out their chests, spread

dark wings. Their breath,
restless gusts of light,
shakes great fir

to their knees; but as I close
my eyes and dream a way
through the darkness of who I am

how many of my totems will fall
like geese shot from the sky?
How many centuries must I sleep?

Life Class (II)

I remember crossing Dean's Yard behind the Abbey, the rain not nearly as grey as the stone walls around me. Inside the immense brick coffin of the Royal Architectural Museum I climbed the worn steps leading up to the School. They were cluttered with broken-nosed martyrs and saints laid out to meet final judgement on comfortless stone couches.

This way, Miss, kindly Mr. Ford nodding me in, his balding head the only point of light in the entire building. *You are the Canadian then? Yes, from the far west,* my tongue caught in my throat like a mouse in a box, *but my father was born in Kent.* A window flew open on an alien wind.

Laughing eyes lit from within, he said, *The School resumes Monday next when last year's fossils have returned from summer hols. Don't frown so, Miss Carr. I shall place you in the life class if that is to your liking.*

INDIAN CHURCH

Side by side we struggle
toward the sky, its clarity
never wholly revealed

to us, its aloofness one more
half-grasped mounting of the mind.
The shadow we each cast

across the other's path
divides its remnant of light
into moments of rich dark earth

where cedars throw themselves
into the deeper certainty
of their spreading roots—

their branches so alive
to the wind who cares
how dimly these trees spring

from dust. The canopy they weave
gives the mission shelter,
allows it time to draw the dark

mantle from the land and build
a haven for it, infuse it
with hymns the Indians

have begun to sing.
The dead wait in their huddled
graves like impatient seeds.

Soon the church will burst;
its walls become the forest walls,
the sea's edge, the wilderness.

Saturday Evening (A Letter To Lawren Harris)

A black fog weighs the earth down;
even the trees are heavy.

All day I found little time to paint
with drains to unclog, dogs to tend,
with eaves to free of abandoned nests,
soggy leaves to rake.

This evening I am numb with silence.
Four walls and my tenants withdraw into themselves
while I sit with a rug at my window.
Even my ravens soar among the rafters with closed beaks.

I long for the slow folding of William's paddle through water,
the sudden rise of poles
against the carbon-hard forest at dawn.
I still hear the voice of D'Sonoqua calling the midnight cats
to her breast for feeding.
I still taste the cedar musk of rain the next morning.

And yes,
I agree all is part of the same whole,
all art is the eternal quest to express
the Soul that dwells within and around us.
But must I make mine your need to fell
God as I know Him, pulling up devotions
rooted in me when I was Small,
Father's soft-eyed, littlest girl,
one hand held firmly in his while entering church,
the other free, clutching a bouquet of maidenhair and lilies,
the hem of my pinafore down?

Still, as Whitman says, *Delve!*
Mould! Pile the words of the earth.
Work on, age after age, nothing is to be lost.

Lawren, my hand is become unsteady,
forgive me.
I am so alone here, such an old fool,
really.

Life Class (III)

I was taken aback when the model stepped nude from the screen. In San Francisco I had worked only from clay busts and women fully dressed. The girl on my left twittered, *You lot from the Colonies should draw only cows.*

The model's skin was clear, shone like milk in the sun. I picked up my chalk. The girl's many stances soon leapt from my paper. *Now rest!* In one movement we all laid our chalk down. Forty minutes wondrously passed.

Guyasdams' D'Sonoqua

I have stood at her feet a long, lone time.
He who carved her cut her
from the tree as from love.
Rising into the dusk, she stands
shifting her weight back and forth
between light and dark, calling,

her lips a gibbous moon,

for his return.
No one heeds her call but I,
and I have come unseen,
hide among the shadows
her eyes cast about

like a little girl
angry over a lost, unwanted doll.
Why the Indians loved her,
feared her,
faced her away from the sea
with outstretched arms

is the wilderness of the forest
she breathed
into the women's loins.
But she herself remained untouched,
snatched the newborn
from their arms.

She does not know herself
says all

in the *Oo-oo-oo-oo*
of her lips,
in her breasts like eagle heads.

I am sister to her childless womb.

Life Class (IV)

I had little time for pride hemmed in by those society girls. Their wasp waists would have snapped if they ever dared to draw breath— and they didn't. Chalk never fell from their fingers. *It's vanished,* they'd shriek, as if Satan had snatched it. How they sniggered at me, scrambling under their easels. *What did she say, Hattie? Lost her what? You should learn proper English, dear child.*

Say CHAULK.

SOPHIE FRANK

One night, while the wind bundled
a small town in snow,
abandoning it like a child in the forest,
birth swept me protesting
into the hungry maw of the storm.

Thirty years later, very much worn,
I found myself sunning on sand
beached like seaweed on the North Shore.
Sophie placid beside me
unknotted her shawl.
With her newest papouse
the afternoon snoozed in her lap.
Nimble fingers of breeze
shook off rings of cloud,
wove our laughter into a plait
supple as the cedar she tore
in strips, coaxed into baskets.

This was the pattern: rising
in the dark ravelled around me
I would catch the first ferry,
let it thread me into the dawn.
Heavy with sleep the Lions yawned,
the two mountain peaks tossing
their heads out of the mist
in fleshy ripples of forest.
The city fell back like ash
tapped from my first cigarette,
the greys dissolving into waves
peeling like skin away from the hull.
Crossing the threshold I found her
braiding her daughter's black hair.

Tea always brewed on the stove.
Licking round its door the flames
knit me a cozy blanket of warmth.

The days it poured we spent quietly
cross-legged on her clean dirt floor.
The summer I met her I sailed north.
At Alert Bay I knelt at Bear's cracked feet,
married myself to the decline of her race.
On my return she puzzled over my sketches.
Raven, she told me, must have rested
his silver beak on my shoulder,
hurled the sun back into the sky,
giving me light.
Rain beat the drum of her house.
Sparked by the lantern sifting shadow
like a rattle over the room,
her eyes kindled flames
that changed from hummingbird to mosquito,
to owl, to otter, to wolf.
One sprang into my right eye—
a squirrel flying between trees.

Sun or rain we seeded our last hour
among the graves the Reserve church
drew to its breast away from the forest.
Flaming on the newly struck match
of her faith, God led Sophie here
to care for her dead. Helping her
push back the weeds choking each stone,
I began learning their names.

Rosie, Tommy, Emily, George—
these last I saw buried with toys
I gave them hugged to their chests.
Twenty-one children fell from her
womb into the arms of the earth.

Alone on the dock Sophie watched
the boat tear away from the moorings,
weave a darkening wake.
Pulled away from the west,
dusk stretching like a shadow behind me,
I felt the wind rise.
Over the far shore
storm clouds opened their jaws.
The city swallowed me whole.

LIFE CLASS (V)

I am sorry, Klee Wyck, Mrs. R. would say whenever I dared to complain about the monsters at the School, *but Canada is vulgar, small despite all its vast space. I am glad I left when I did, though Mr. Redden just buried. A good place to be born in, but to die there is poor taste. I wanted Freddie raised with a decorous mind.*

What about the tremendous forests, I'd retort, *that can root deep in a child's heart? Or the mountains? Or the rivers that pour the heart-song of our origins through their mouths? You were born there, Mrs. R.! How can you dismiss its sweeping breath? How I despise London, its history muddled, one building snuggled up to the next like pigs in a sty. Even your parks are glutted with people. They never admire the trees, just the statues.*

Then I'd fall silent. What I thought of the British Museum and their galleries stuffed with mummies and old masters who copied each other I kept to myself.

Nothing new in art for hundreds of years.

BIG RAVEN

Your stubborn dark
folds its wings above me,
allowing light

to strain through the sky's
bruised lattice of cloud,
its shafts glimmering

pillars of rain.
The cedars
in banks of sea-green flame

crest nearer your breast.
The forest your people cut
away in strips from the shore

heals over fishing camps
they one by one have abandoned.
Proud bird, spread your wings

across the light and trick
change in this, its voracious
game of decay. Spread your wings,

make me the thunder
flowing to their pinions,
their span bridging the ache

of the sun changing horizon.

LIFE CLASS (VI)

It pained me to enter the School. My last day a young man sat hunched on a great flag at the door. As I passed my cloak brushed his elbow. He glanced up. *Such wonderful towers, what?* He was scribbling down the squashed contours of the Westminster slum. *For charlatans,* I said, the carved door to the School banging numbly behind me.

BLUNDEN HARBOUR

I

there is an absence of red

a raven hovers above me
his shadow closes over the inlet

I want to leave before dawn
and wonder if
the boatman will pass
back through the entrance

I sit on the rotting dock

behind me three totems lurch
elongated human bodies
their bellies swelling with wet

the years stand apart

I have preserved them in charcoal
preserved the moss
nesting in their cracking joints

they lean uneasily
their bellies heaving

we are waiting for the boatman to come

II

I am never certain of the boatman's return

on this island like all
others I visit
the Indians left before

he carried me here grudgingly
piloting the narrow inlet
his head tucked close to his chest
like one asleep and visiting
the land he was born in
and cannot remember

he prefers the nightmare
that lies outside
what I capture on paper

he fears the darkness he forsook

how the world will interpret
the world I have entered

he fears what I disturb

III

I have been on this island for an age

I cannot remember where I was born
when the sun last rose
when the boatman left

I have pillaged graves for weapons
stripped brittle rags off corpses

I hunt the darkness for warmth

the raven visits me
bringing me sleep

I am one of his children

he burnt my sketches with his breath
with the cinders I darken
the lines unwrinkling my belly

he teaches me what must be remembered

the importance of darkness

IV

my eyes squint

the mountains' tall outline
is green with dawn

I feel my belly seething

the boatman glides in
the rising sun dipping
glinting in the blade
of his paddle

the totem nearest me
raises his arm

fist clenched

the water reddens

LIFE CLASS (VII)

Klee Wyck, you have sat there without one word of bile tippling off your tongue for almost ten minutes. Pass me one more slice of plum cake and tell us another of your Indian tales, Sammy Blake winked, sat back in his chair, his whiskers resuming their usual distance from my cheek. He took Sunday tea with us often. Like Mrs. R. he was born in Quebec. A bit of Canada still peeped out of him at me.

Old George, I mumbled, thrilled all eyes raced to mine like a crow toward rings placed on a sill, *was grieved his brother had drowned, his watery grave unmarked. He paddled his canoe from the Ucluelet dock, a silhouette wobbling against the moon, just as the sky and ocean conspired to drag it below the horizon. You will never believe what he had with him. A marble cross he pulled up from the church-yard. I saw him like Christ with it straddling his back. I rallied the spinster missionaries and we chased after. The three of us stood on the dock, the whole village around us and laughing. Suddenly he paused. The moon snuffed itself out. In the dark we heard a great splash. Everyone thought he had suicided. Then we heard the alcoholic dip of his paddle coming nearer, then—*

Good God, Klee Wyck, Sammy whooped, *he threw the cross in!* The whole tea party guffawed with him and I must admit I let loose a few loud hoots and snuffles. *My dear Klee Wyck,* Mrs. R. said, breath-less as she waved me to hot up her cup, *the natives named you well;*

it means 'laughing one' doesn't it?

NIRVANA

Whatever is held
inside the forest's coal-
dark heart was barely

carved into the felled
trees the Indians raised
before the wood began

swelling with rain,
the finely wrought
distinctions peeling away

like stars from the sky.
The thickening grain
pushes the heart farther in,

readies it for the perfect
blankness between
darkness and light.

How I wish time
would stop,
the forest fall back.

I would carve all hearts
free of their prisons of rot,
hold them high in the sun,

their winged shapes each
a calyx of diamond
unfolding petals of light.

The Totems Permit Me Peace

At first, I only woke the fleeting
glimmer behind the land's weathered
face, not the vacant
silence of its
stare. I merely observed, with sleight of hand
and colour, how the stubbled curve of its chin
dropped into the ocean like a seagull's
sudden cry into the wind. I never asked myself
why.

The light I knew then was not
local.
The etiquette of gardens
and shuttered windows skirted all questions
the veins of granite and cedar posed.
When exposed by some new
foundation, by another road
pushing aside the forest musk,
the land's raw colour was muted by delicate
webs of alyssum, day-lilies, and primroses.

Then the darkness fell: what light there was
I needed. My brush thirsted,
groped free of the decorum my race mapped out.
Its bristles felt out paths all forests lead
into themselves. I made the journey
up the Inside Passage to Alert Bay, then painted
Skeena, Kitwancool, Skidegate, Masset,
half-deserted villages built on rock
that formed my backbone.

But what I cannot let go of permits me
my art: my little griffon dog
asleep on my knees, the plait of lavender
stowed among my dry clothes
while I camp, the packet of tea biscuits
I keep as treats in my carpet coat bag.

At dusk, after William's left me
alone on the island,
after I've sketched, surveyed the poles,
they recede into darkness,
become one with the forest.
I listen like all Indians before me
for the land's voice:
the hoot-owl,
the raven's wing,
the claw-print,
the salmon-call.
Its absence inhabits me,
a limpid series of echoes that blurs into night
like waves through salt water.
With the fear of God that Father gave me
I pray for His blessing.
The totems permit me peace.

II

Having exhausted Indian themes, Emily turns to the forest.

Nothing stands alone; each is only a part. A picture must be a portrayal of relationships.

GREY

Harris said: *Cast*
your Indian stuff aside,
find totems of your own.
And I did,
for he spoke
what I had left
unspoken in my heart.
When the forest was dry enough
I edged my way
down between the boles,
found solace
in the water-soft quiet.

And here I am again,
a latecomer this spring
to Heaven's gate,
the forest a tinderbox
locked against me.
A heavy mail of darkness
chains the cedars.
They cannot move.
Even their branches
won't ease back,
let me pass.
I could stand before them
a thousand years,
never know I'm here.

Sit on your camp-stool,
old fool, and think.
Get out your journal,
think a way in
between the trees.

These cedars are older
than Adam.
God had no voice and spoke only
in forms.
                    'Forest', 'tree',
cones overlapping and wrapped
in darkness, impenetrable
as one's heart.
Now, drawn to the forest edge,
I am one of His thoughts—

It's almost dawn.
The first light rolls
off the cedars.
They shimmer, wet
windows, turn black-
green.
          That little pine
in the foreground,
the first and last of this race,
could be the centre.
It shines from within:
bronze light cracks through
its crust of darkness,
a grey beacon.
                    It draws me
into its cave.
I shall
burn there, untouched, unborn,
outside memory.

RED CEDAR

How I wish the years
could be like this

reaching upward
unwavered
by notions of sky

I need such days

all limbs at ease
in the wind's sway

like wings

MOTHER WAS GENTLE

She never wore pearls.
When strong enough

she would rise from her sick bed,
tuck us in,
her fingers at rest on our foreheads,
her fingers a moment of warmth,

her eyes lit by the coal lamp
brightening the side of my bed

until she blew the flame out,
the smoke from the wick
a lullaby her breath drew from her lips,
her leaning forward lost to the dark,
I don't ever remember her
closing the door.

Maybe once I heard her

skirt brushing the floorboards
as she crossed
the hall to her room.
Whenever I think of it
I am still twelve

falling asleep with a doll
I seldom cared for
strangely content in my arms.
A mother had let her
face melt in the sun.

Mother's dying was like the grapevine
Father would tend.

It overwhelmed one side of the house.
He named it Isabella.
I resented him, thought he loved
her every twist more than Mother,
more than myself. I was wrong,

now know as Mother knew
the comfort he found in pruning,
each cut giving shape
to Isabella's dark curves.

I wish Mother had told me.

Such knowledge is climbing
too late with unruly limbs
about the rooms of my flesh.
No longer young,
long used to sitting alone

here under this alder
in Father's praying chair—
sternly sighing *amen*
as it always did under his weight—

I examine each twist of vine
in the leaf-
mottled light of my afternoon

garden where my dogs
cavort like children,
chasing their tails.
Remembering that time,
what little I know of it

is a tangle of growth
and dead wood.

Like Isabella's fruit
its ripeness is sour,
such bruised skin
soon to collapse inward,
wrinkle round darkness.

Mother was gentle,
was Father's reflection,

her grey eyes fine steel.
Strong enough once
she took me, his truant,
into the forest.
We picnicked, the two of us,

all afternoon.
I made daisy chains
while every moment she hemmed,
with straight seams,
broad folds of linen
into a stiff apron for Small.

We both wore daisies.

We smiled secretly at high tea
when we got home.

Mother was so gentle
and now I am old.

OLD TREE AT DUSK

Wind stiffens

in these flagging branches
tagging
their valediction to the evening's
blue web of sky,

an endless dark

shift, a garment of darkening
dew falling
softly to earth.
I can't stand even this

gentle weight draping

even one shadow over my shoulder,
sensing as I must
the days shorten. The years
recede from my fingers,

an intricate braille

embroidered on the luminous
air we so seldom
breathe until it is too late.
What secrets do I feel

fall open

inside my clumsy lungs?
Something tingles like dawn.
An old tree can only
just sense the slow pulse

of sap draining

to its roots one last time.
Proud to the tip of each needle
an old tree raises the night
wind to its uppermost branch,

its very last ensign.

BOXING DAY, 1934

Night was still close as I set out
for Christmas matins. Everything dark and mysterious,
the air damp with rain. Kitchen windows cast one,
perhaps two thin patches of light
on what remained of a week's quiet snow.
Puddles gleamed under street lamps, road after road,
the shadow of my umbrella my companion the whole way.
A procession of fir trees may have followed.
It was too dark to know.

There is something holy about communion before the sun
shifts into morning. Something warm and ephemeral,
hidden in the Cathedral's dim corners.
Yesterday the scent of pine wreaths, the scarlet of berries,
the star-shapes of the altar poinsettias,
wove into the carols, into the bishop's soft litanies.

> *We three kings of Orient are;*
> *bearing gifts we traverse afar.*

In a single voice the whole congregation rose,
a single wave inspirited with joy.

When we came out the dawn came also.
Wet and grey. The street lamps were off;
I walked home alone, my umbrella weighted with rain.
Most curtains were still drawn,
tired by the bustle of Christmas Eve shopping.

> *Westward leading, still proceeding,*
> *guide us to thy perfect light.*

This evening, after straightening the four red candles
my dear sisters placed in my window two nights before,
I relit them, though they were almost burned down.

EDGE OF THE FOREST

The forest is Job.
God said: *The loggers shall*
reduce thee to bracken.
The great trees fell back,
rank after rank,
leaving a long succession
of stumps, ragged mouths
turned to the sky.

Where the fir cones fell
seedlings take root.
Birds return.
Then the animals.
Salal and oregon grape
fall back to thickening
trunks.
Centuries pass.

It is mid-morning.
The wind a chill hand
nests in the small
of my back.
The edge of the forest
has just rushed up
to a swath cut
close to the roots
of an ancient fir left
standing, its long
branchless trunk
lancing its crown
falling from the sky.

The fir strains higher,
higher, asking: *Why
am I still here?*
God says: *You are what
I measure time by.*
The wind threads sun
through its crown
like blood.

TWO SKETCHES OF SAN FRANCISCO

I

Light and Dark

After Father's death I found myself
pursuing art for the first time
as an artist, the School jammed
into a low room over Pine Street Market.
Pure vegetable, the air breathing
through the floorboards enveloped me
in leaves of green and tender being.

From above came warmth. A window
in the ceiling embraced the sun,
its brush sweeping across the room,
brightness changing with the season.
Underneath I worked, sketching fruit
bought below and reaping growth.
Not wanting love, my heart ripened.

Such an unusual scent freedom has;
one day I found mine wholly rotted.
My sisters came to visit for a year,
bringing rain. Brother Richard followed,
dying, needing warmth. Life stilled,
its half-guessed-at fruits rearranged.
The rooms of my young body darkened.

II

Dark and Light

Twenty-five years later I took rooms
across the Bay, worked in Chinatown
painting lanterns for a hotel ballroom.
Money earned chalked up with money saved
I managed an eight-month stay, my life
rearranged, Hill-House boarded up,
some tenants wintering with my sisters.

The change in climate I rejoiced in,
sketched a little, shopped, my basket
laden with strange Chinese pastries,
dried black mushrooms, passion fruit.
For days an orchid flamed in my window,
the petals soon loosened by the wind,
privates defrocked, stamens missing.

One day, walking near Union Square,
I chanced on an old beau, Mayo Paddon.
I spotted his name engraved on a brass
plate mounted at his office entrance.
A youth who shared with me a love
for God, he followed me to England
twenty years before, pleading marriage.

The man I met across his desk dropped
moist eyes, his desiccated fingers spread
on the blotter like stilled fan blades.
His voice cut my flesh. I felt godless,
a grape parched on the vine. He said
his wife had left him. I requested car
fare, my cash dissipated at the Market.

His love letters I burned years before.
Writing London, he hoped life without him
wasn't barren. The man would have wizened
me till my spirit hardened. Each Christmas
I receive his greetings, the card unsigned.
I put down my brush, turn off the light,
smell the everlasting pressed inside.

FOREST, BRITISH COLUMBIA

More than one way in

into the forest. For instance
light carves
through a dense shell of cedar crowns,
its teeth gnawing

lower dark

branches into smooth dark scrolls,
into nimbus clouds
brightening over my head as I pass beneath,
any change in light

delicious

scent drawing me deeper
into opening
a path through undergrowth knit
closely to

the forest

heart, the swords of each fern
each whetted on
the stone cold of the need I always find
myself carrying. I look up: branches

sharp and interwoven

against a lightening sky—
I can never
separate what continues to exist ...
Light falls over branches

curtain upon curtain

such lace the finest
needlework in all creation.
Its net harvests my dark,
smooths it into these wet

trees finding

a way into where I can see,
the forest like myself a fragment
of God, once unnamed,
now a leviathan suddenly gentle,

suddenly waking.

JACK-IN-THE-PULPIT REMEMBERED

Seventeen floors above the first thaw
griming Manhattan, I was introduced
to Miss Georgia O'Keeffe, the fugitive
grey walls of the gallery holding us
for a moment under the arresting
bell of one of her dilating flowers.

Terse in an expensive black dress,
she barely spoke, draped herself
sparingly over the supportive arm
of a courtly, much greyer old man;
hours later I apprized he was some
great photographer, her husband.

Freeing himself, he charmed me all
round the room, critting her work.
One canvas, a jack-in-the-pulpit,
swept me into its indigo vortex
of petals, promises swiftly opening
around me concentric circles of wake.

I nearly drowned, the calm within
suddenly uncentred, giddy, turning
me away from the edge; years later,
trees parting toward this focusing
coast, I ache to wash myself through
one endless conduit of essence.

TREE

Inside the ring
of trees sounds the hour,

its trunk a soft luminous bell.
Count the lines loosened

gently from my face,
the ripples sent quickly

from the tree's heart.
Time is a sudden stone

falling into such
a fluid cradle of roots.

Who would believe these harmonies?
Count their rings of growth.

MOTHERING SUNDAY (A LETTER TO CAROL PEARSON)

Your card arrived on time, Baboo, as usual.
The mother wren on the front feeds her young,
chirrups at the tulips opening like mouths
beside her on the mantel. Last night hard rain
seeded the garden; cedars puffed up in the wind.
This morning torn-off branches feathered the grass;
the city cracked night's shell, let in today's warmth.

As drawn broke Lizzie laid a wreath on Mother's grave,
camelias brightening against the weathered stone,
dew exhaled on petals I am sure by now are wilted.
Like buds, once picked, our time is brief. We open,
find ourselves arranged in life's strange bouquet,
cuttings of unique shades and breeds. Look at me.

And you child, with a wanton smile, long ago
you bloomed into more than a visitor to my studio.
Brush clenched, you would settle at my table,
beginning to hum, the lesson I set you at last
within range, faltering lines magically scored
on the page. I'd say rest and we would laugh,
hurry down to the ocean with our evening snacks.
Countless times the sunset loosened its petals
over us before all was gone, the remaining crusts
tossed to gulls. Nestled between logs I repeated
stories about Small, wished on stars that rained
down like sparks. My whole life I had extinguished
much for art. Chasing after you I found myself
playing tag through the lightly falling dark.

You are a woman now, with a child and husband.
Remember yourself in part as the little girl
who tucked her way in under the wing of a house
ready to settle like a hen on an eggless nest.
For seven years a room snug beneath the eaves
was yours, just blocks away from where parents
who loved you lived in a white frame house,
lived and loved you enough to nourish a young
heart's need for an old woman with two parrots,
a cherry tree, dogs, and a choice of paints.

Memories pause like geese nearing water,
the season's face mirrored among dying reeds.
Though I miss you, child, pay your Mum no heed.

Woo

Monkey in a tree:
tiny human hands,
canny human feet,
a snake-tongue tail
curling smugly
through the branches.

And that dress!
How dirty it looks
against the dew-fresh sky.
Twigs have tugged its bow,
rent its skirt,
its threads,
red,
gold,
gunny-sack brown,
spill like leaves
into the wind.

O Woo,
your eyes are slit walnuts.
Tell me
what do you see,
dancing along your branch,
nose like a child's
pressed against glass.

An apple?

An earwig?

Quiet now and tell me
all in a hug
right here in my arms.
Even the pine needles shudder,
rattled free
by your chatter.

Quiet now.
Are you watching me
watch you?

III

Emily discovers a style of her own.

Inspiration is intention obeyed.

METCHOSIN SKETCHING TRIP

After a night rain birds are the first memory
of sun, giddy yellows flitting under my eyelids.

Late dawn's brush bristles with soft musks,
sweeps over the clearing, tickles the loose

skin of my caravan: the old elephant wakes.
A stowaway in its heart, I am Mrs. Noah

rising from bed. Like my creatures I delight
in my hunger. From my window puddles spread;

in them I glimpse the sinuous calligraphy
of branches the wind writes and erases.

ABOVE THE TREES

The sky,

its half-completed fan
spread, anticipates
the radiance of each cedar's
feathered crown.

The earth spins east,
the sky west.
How still they are

as I lie here, refreshed,
pinned among the currents
by the earth's
whirling

into tindery night.
Fiddleheads,
pebbles shivering down this
chilly stream,

ignite my skin;
twigs trailing
just above my face—
the shadows of small leaves
tracing its shape
like spots in time—

flit off,
skittish as wasps.

As the sun
rides the last wave of its
flood higher
my eyes blur together.

Minutes are thread like beads.
One after the other

the cedars flare,

the final branches abandoning
themselves to
the fiery blue of the sky's

opposing gyre.

PORTENTS

I

Father thought himself God.
I saw this in late childhood
and rebuked him, though he said
the God lording above us
shared with him a harshness.

I met this God in Tregenna Wood,
knew no way to approach Him,
awestruck as I was among trees
descending like the Host
over low hills into St. Ives,
its ancient buildings and streets
posing atop cliffs for art
students more patient than I;
the rough basalt, pleated,
dropping into the Bristol Channel,
a seamless curtain of light.

Among the moss-winged trees
I rested my eyes—forests
at Ucluelet remembered as shadow
falling back from clearings
where missionaries spread tea.
I touched the flank of an oak,
my hand coated with resin,
broad leaves fringing the sky.

In a shallow depression I knelt.
Long used to fearing God
I mixed a dark palette,
drew Him all-seeing yet unseen,
His auguries stitched on an arras
of ivy and ponderous branches.
It seemed a touch Catholic.

I turned away from my board.
In a tumult of wind Talmage appeared,
hands in his pockets.
One of my teachers,
he examined the sketch,
prepared fresh paint.
His careful brushwork parted my darkness.
In poured light, its advent balanced
on the tip of a leaf.

II

Realization at Crécy-en-Brie.
Pleased with my progress,
Harry Gibb repainted the scene on my easel.
Something entirely other roared
out of that hedgerow of poplars,
shaking the linked crowns—
the human snagged in the hot
wave of chartreuse he dashed
across the cool face of the sky.

This passion I never forgot,
soon found bits of myself
unexpectedly mixed into my sketches
as I worked his strange colours
day after day in the warm fields.
With its vision of light,
the New Art, having drawn me
like a pilgrim to France,
put a match to my darkness.

Trivia slowly fell away
from my rhythms like leaves,
the branches single brushstrokes,
the whole overrun by a force
that, once fathomed,
would carry me back to my West,
a force I hoped could snare
the land's unpaintable spirit.
With sacrifice, Gibb said,
mine would be a strength someday
grown into one among the century's
great—a woman, a painter.
Such praise I could not have
imagined, a rocket he sent
tearing straight into Heaven.

One day I rose into the hills
overlooking St. Efflame;
below Britanny spread its coast
out like a sun-lit fan,
England hidden, I mused,
behind a fog of tradition.
In the foreground I sketched in
an old peasant so like Father,
his brow retaining the Godhead,
gold the soft pride of his smile.

III

Spirit and the wilderness ...
When Mark Tobey arrived
fresh from Paris on the Seattle ferry
I had felt abandoned for years,
a paste solitaire in Victoria's
steel-claw setting,
isolation hooking deep into my flesh.
People smirked
at my pram full of animals
while I shopped,
another of the Carr antiques
pottering all around town—
this one trying her darnedest,
Lizzie said, to spatter our late
father's honour with paint.

Slowly I was beginning to heal:
the words 'Group of Seven'
and 'holy' sweet on my tongue;
the totems I sketched that summer
bivouacked all over the Charlottes
imbued with a forest stillness
I ached so much to get at.
Wrenching me, with little ruckus,
away from an eternity of housework,
Mark handed me a camel-hair brush.
In my studio he held court,
the assembled steeped each night
in his epiphanies in France.
He talked of the manipulation
of light and perspective,
the latent power of objects
suddenly transfigured by space.

His ideas took me aback.
A totem mother and babe
rose out of my darkness,
an interior light I had only
guessed at housed in her loins;
her hands so full with love
I made them huge and distorted
as they enfolded the child,
his face wise as a father
of fathers, a talisman
of all that is given,
lost, found, and forgiven.

Quiet fell the evening inside me,
my life striations of cloud
at last lifting away from the moon.
The heart of the forest thrown open before me,
I approached overwhelmed,
myself a daughter of prayer
conceived by Father in Mother,
for God's pleasure,
at the edge of the world.

SCORNED AS TIMBER, BELOVED OF THE SKY

Suddenly in this clearing at the forest centre,
climbing the endless finger of this
lone fir with my eyes,
it is enough to watch
expanding circles of light
wave out from behind the tree's crown.

SUNDAY AFTERNOON (A LETTER TO LAWREN HARRIS)

Have not slept well all week,
kept waking to the wind
chastening branches that screen my window.
Was Lazarus chafing at insomnia,
its hand clammy on my brow.

Thought this morning what the use—
rose early and walked to church,
found comfort in the responses,
the prayerful bond God contracts with Man.
Bunched humbly on the altar
daffodils—those immortal flowers—
drank up light the organ spilled
from its pipes, their thrilled faces opened wide.
My heart burst its dam, sang and sang.

Is singing now,
my back unstiffening against a log
the sea tucked under cliffs below Dallas Road.
Waves fold into shore like wings;
mountains across the strait
flash, craggy amethysts,
an ancient crown of thorns.
Here, against sun-bleached wood,
my bones at last are warm,
want no quarrel with God
who walks toward me like a friend.

Lawren, you too have been my guide,
unfolding another map of the forest,
your studied route a code my heart,
flagging, has been slow to follow—
my range better suited to hymns
learned in the front pew on Father's knee.

For my critic Christ's passion;
my heart rhapsodic at the sea's edge—
someday I hope to wake, rest in Heaven.

Laughing Forest

The arbutus delirious—

summer's skin burst
back from flame
upon flame
of flame-licked trunks;
the new leaves
nimble,
eluding the wind
with their lucid green.

Like the wind
I once
imagined
years would fall into the currents
                like leaves.

        Like the wind
        I imagined.

        I saw each leaf whisked
                            singly
        to earth.
        All branches
        a stripped glow,
        I hunched into the wind's
        vortex,

        forgot utterly,
        spun in its dusk-ridden eye.

Then suddenly I knew

the abandon of years.

Under my limber
feet, leaves
of less
riotous trees kindle.

My arbutus leaves spark in the air.

I turn and I turn.

In my cheek I feel
the cells of my blood uniting

rampant as fireworks.

GOLDSTREAM FLATS

Oblivious to death my dogs mate,
Maybbe's tongue lolling, the old girl one with the joining.

I melt into the sun.
The breezes flush hot clouds into the sky.

Such a delicious somersault quickening the flesh.
A sun shower floods cracks veining the earth.

Monkey Woo plays at my feet,
her spinster hands hugging a week-old pup to her breast.

The days swell like droplets of sweat on my brow.
Under my cot slumber a month's sketches fecund with wonder.

WOOD INTERIOR

Light a sea-green cave

opens above me.
Trees
shine through, warm
children of light joined

to a sky

I never quite fathom.
These trees
may never cut themselves loose
and root in the earth.

I wake whenever I am.

Boughs swim round me like astonished fish.
Salal
in soft currents whispers
delight in my ear.

Wet

hung between the trees weaves
a hammock beneath me.
A salt wind hums me asleep.
Such bliss this

salmon dream.

SWIRL

a single breath

sifts its
branch of light across
the next
        breath
emerald
     sa
ffron
     o
      l
       i
        v
         e

      r u s t

    each tree
    an axis
    of
      sun

the wind funnels

three
hundred
feet

through bark

into concentric
circles of my
heart
      a shimmering

      veil of
      cedar sweeps over

two stumps

across tiny pines
sucking
them into the forest's lungs

FULL MOON

Jade, turf, myrtle, bice, sage—
the forest invites me in.

Two pebbles settle in the crotch
around a root bright with pitch.

Far into a cedar a hollow spreads,
soft light bleeding from within.

SUNSHINE AND TUMULT

And finally, like God newborn,

you shake your plumes
across the wind-
strung sun
farther and farther

like fingers of an outstretched hand

and stir
the afternoon into giddy
tremblings

so brief

the whole forest murmurs,
one wave
deeper into the next,

the aftershock of your light.

316 BECKLEY STREET

It is a woman's room, my old studio;
this morning for the last time
I woke there, its gestation
hours later given over to new owners—
my emptied heart fruiting strange growth.

A few blocks away I unpack in this cottage.
One by one the rooms dress in my habits.
The dusky windows soften with lace.
Clutter gentles the cupboards.
The first dishes drain in the sink.

One door I cannot make myself open,
though it leads to an easel and paints:
the days ahead not yet my birthright—
the woman I am: a sketch my shy hands,
when ready, will flesh into life.

ABOVE THE GRAVEL PIT

A sea up here—

bottomless and stirring,
its clarity
unclouded blue
                    tearing—
waves of
heat sweating

over the horizon's kindled brow.
Bits

of me pop

up, leaves sprung
higher
on the currents' smooth knuckles.

Others snag

on twigs,
each skeleton of veins held
lightly,

the sun's detritus.

The earth breathes,
its force treading air year
upon year.
Why

has my heart never
hovered so

brightly,

wet wings unstiffening

above the earth's
gravelly mouth?

Lizzie's Death

The door to Mother's sewing room drifts open.
Here, in a corner, my first easel stood.

At age seven I fashioned it from branches
Father gleaned from the back hedge.

Hunched on chairs draped with afternoon light
Alice and I stitch our last sister's shroud.

Two old maids among nine children
we coddle the dead. Creation busies our hands—

soft linen yielding to thread,
gleaming needles joining panels of absence.

STRAIT OF JUAN DE FUCA

The sea is cedar dust.

I root myself down
into the cliffs,
into a twisting spray

of gorse sticky
with dew.
          Blind shards
of sun
break like an egg

over the mountains,
soften into fire-gold

crescents that melt
into shore.

I root myself down,

permit night
to drift up from the sea
like kelp,
stretch itself out.

Some days
I walk out to these cliffs,
sit down,

let the sun strain

through my thoughts
like dampness through cloth;

someday I will join them,
wrap myself in them,

walk out to sea.

IV

Spirit burdened by illness and old age, Emily looks further inward.

*In a grey woollen gown under the scarlet
blankets with pillows at my back and hot
bottle at my feet, I find the earth lovely.
Autumn does not dismay me any more than
the early winter of my body. Some can live
to a great age but enjoy little. I have lived.*

Saint Joseph's Hospital, 1937

My heart, a knot undone with pain, forgot
a beat, the message cut. I lie awake,
my life in jars of paint. The thirst I slake
with tears is loss, a canvas stretched too taut
by years misspent, the will of God I thought
assuaged and framed. Totemic fir now break
through mist and gulp the dusk in draughts. I shake
with breath. A month of pain has cast my lot.

I lie awake. To live, the Doctor said,
the trees and sky must rest. My pain must rest.
A breeze afire with shades of summers past
now scents my room. Machine aloft my bed
I type them out, neglected coasts so blessed
with myth, the poles I sketched. They hold me fast.

MASSET BEARS

Cornered by evening sun slanting
darkness across them
two bears graven in cedar

snarl in salal rising
inside the well of the forest.
Long ago their carver,

one with his blade, saw them leap
from the dark, rear up on hind legs.
Though each crack now slitting them open

is riddled with rot,
the awe voiced in the wood
still can be heard.

MONDAY MORNING (A LETTER TO LAWREN HARRIS)

I had a visitor last night.
He came unannounced and in from the cold,
a solitary warmth flushing his cheeks
as Nurse hung up his worn, weary raincoat.

She sat him by the fire and served us tea.
This man with hands folded
comfortably over one knee
would lean closer, then back,
his voice so gentle it stirred me
like a breeze through branches
too long becalmed, hopelessly tangled.

Very soon I found myself talking about Small,
revealing her love for lilies that would unfurl
light quite suddenly through grass.
Each spring Small picked them in the one
field Father never had
ploughed and remade as England.
My pictures, he says, have loosed
her love for things wild,
knocking down the snake fence
choking it back.
                        Drawn into the riot
that livened my exhibition this fall
he felt the wide sweep of my brush
underline the whole of this coast;
by sharing it with others
he says I plant Eden in soil
enriched by my original field.

Goodness, I said,
then to myself, *Who is this man?*
I studied his face: straightforward
features planed to softness by youth.
They are now written over by the first
lines of age accentuating the grain.
Under a high forehead is hewn
a nose that curves to a mouth
smooth-lipped and grinning.
Two eyes balance the whole;
dark blue, they sound the deep
talk of the forest.

Unsettled by the quiet forming
over the evening, he broke it,
edging his chair nearer the fire.
He was brimming with questions about the stories I sent him,
at Ruth's urging, a few weeks before.
I had forgotten them,
all worry fallen asleep in the arms
of our heart-to-heart talk.
Rubbing my eyes like a child
suddenly roused, I stammered
that the prod of my pen
across paper has unearthed
more of the past than I want,
my prose being quite loose,
most of it gravel. He laughed.
Leaning a touch closer
he shyly offered me help.

He is a Mr. Dilworth.
Ira. I call him Eye.

STORY DRAFT

I was a landlady a long time.
It seems I never did enough dusting,
was grouchy, often mean with the meals.
I hung my totems and trees in the hallways.
On occasion I found my epiphanies
knocked askew, turned to the wall.

My studio I made a room of my own.
I hoisted chairs to each corner
on a homemade rigging of pulleys
and string. Beneath them I worked;
their cobwebbed backs would shimmer
like wings, angels patiently watching.
Worthwhile visitors I would bless,
quickly offer a seat. The fools
I let stand, hoping they'd leave.

One day, before it struck me
my work was at all known,
I heard a knock at my door.
My hair in a kerchief,
my painting dress smelling of turps,
I found on the steps a creature
jazzed up in a great hat,
face hidden under a flutter of ribbons.
You must be the painter, Miss Emily Carr,
it is suggested, cocking head and hat
to the right. It wanted to buy.
Fearing a weakness for posies
drooping under the weight of pastel,
I ushered it in.

What catches your eye, I ventured.
Trees, it said,
branches adrift in the wind.
I pulled out a canvas.
It was taken aback.
I pulled out some sketches.
Seeing God in each one,
it oohed and it aahed,
collapsed into a chair
dropped without warning behind it.
Removing its hat, a woman's eyes
looked straight into mine.
Finally she chose four little pines
I worked hard at stirring
aware of the forest moving in
on cats' feet behind them.

Ten dollars in my pocket
and the woman rehatted, I hurried her out.
My tenants suspiciously eyed
the brown square of paper tucked under her arm.

That night I feted my sisters well on pork loin.

SMALL'S COW SONG

O cow, your eyes
are wide as sunrise.
They wink me
inside your mouth.
Hiho!

Mother likes clover
but not to munch.
I like mine with tea
and milk. Father has no
time for cuddle.

My sisters won't wear
jerseys itchy
as your tongue.
Won't burp your rag-
doll tail. Don't pout.

Your calf cleaned
my face happy ever
after lunch. Do clouds sit
up straight? Rain gets
dirty when it falls down.

I love your hopscotch yard
of puddles. Splash!
That stone's my marker.
Hen combs me toes. Are there
pictures in the gravel?

Cow, your pasture gate
creaks me into bed.
Owl snores me
prayers.
Moo my candle out.

THE LAUGHING BEAR

Turning his back
he refuses me
his eyes.

What does he see
fixed as he is
above the changing
shape of trees?

Does his forepaw shield
his eyes from the final
arrows of mist,
or simply from the rising
sun like a hat brim?

Or is it a shell
cocking his ear
to the wind?—
He's laughing.
Fool!

Have I spoken aloud?
Bear,
old age unwisely loosens
the tongue like a breeze
that shakes the last
berries over the first
layer of snow.
Remember how the Indians
greeted you like spring?
They wrapped you
in a robe of fresh cedar,
sat you down, an elder,
beside the chief's fire.

Turn around you raggy mop.
Look me straight
in the eye.

You carried a warrior's wife
into the forest one night.
They say she married you,
bore twin cubs.

Bear, speak to me.
The quiet is deafening.

Tell me, was it
her husband who carved
you, raised you
so high in the sky?
You laugh, hah!

Your rigid flesh,
his wooden grief.

East Anglia Sanitorium, 1903:
A Recurring Dream

And now have I come to be in this place?
I am awake. The slow breakfast mist scuffs
down the rough halls before me this morning.
I don't know my way. A blank arm, toughened
with starch, locks round my waist, rides me into
the sun's din, chatter of spoon against cup.

I remember him best when day is at rest,
alone on the terrace, the fallen leaves
powdered by wind, his face loose in a grin,
intently in prayer. How great was his need:
I turned him away. From health and England
he fled. My art bears not love, only greed.

Mayo, when we met again in London, you were
a stern bit of Canada stiff on the platform,
the twill of your coat swollen with cold
nights off Ucluelet, the salt of each storm
chiselled in the earnest curve of your chin.
You followed me here. My answer was firm.

And yes, to kill does kill the killer most.
My body transforms itself. The lines
of girlhood insinuate my face.
Three years I denied what our God sanctioned.
Three years I watched my art blossom. Why must
I think of you after such a long time?

FORSAKEN

Driving a path up
through this cavern of trees
a solitary pole glances

off the sun like a fist.
Is blinded.
Many years it sensed

only darkness in the flood
of undergrowth teased
by breezes eddying past.

After shaking their shadows
cryptically open
like fans day after day

wave upon wave of weightless
green flame snapped
back suddenly in a tide

away from the pole—
its eyes having gleaned nothing.
My eyes are wet,

the sun a sham sacrament
of dew collecting this morning
where as I sit exposed

among the roots of a great tree
I am looking up into such
a painfully blue fragment of sky.

No one is blessed.
As the wind leans deeper into
the forest-calm the pole shivers.

How many more years must I
watch fall,
waste into this insubstantial

blotter of earth,
so helpless am I in this,
the diminishing shift of my flesh?

HARO STRAIT

Damn these skittish feet.
They whine with each step,
carry me towards cliffs
where the ocean lies
out cold in the heat.
I must sit
a moment and rest.

Ah ... how I love the sun,
how it beats down
through the branches
like soft rain.
I must write Dilworth,
tell him how the cedars
wake to light.
Sometimes they are cold blue,
then green, sometimes yellow-
warm as their boughs turn into wind.
As they are lost
in the shadow Mount Douglas
draws from the ocean
across them, do they
feel it as darkness
or simply the sun's absence?
Do they feel the tug
of Your love, O My God?
I am your child.
My paintings show that.
But I am also Small,
my father's child,
with knots in my hair.

The little girl trotting
behind him, my fingers
clutching at his coattail,
or cringing at his voice
raised like a hand.
His shadow lengthens
behind me as I limp
to my death.
With each step its grip
nips at my ankle,
a knot jerking taut.
I must write Dilworth:
Eye, Small says she remembers
the Brutal Telling well,
was barely fourteen,
had outgrown herself,
was soon called Milly.
Speak Small while Eye is still
willing to listen.
Mister Ira, Emily wants
you to know about one day
in late spring, the last
trees come into flower.
Mother was dying.
Father and I had gone
for a walk along Dallas Road.
The sea below us stretched
to the world's edge.
'Small,' he said, 'it is time
I warned you how a man
makes a child in a woman.'

'They marry,' I said brightly,
pleased that I already
knew. He started
to laugh. 'No,
pretty whelp,' he said,
gently cuffing my ear,,
'there are many brats
like you whose fathers
were sailors. Navvies
who bedded their mothers,
left the next morning.
One week of shore leave
could make a man a father
seven times over, I know,
I too was a sailor.'
I tried to run away,
Mister Ira, but Father
grabbed at my frock.
It ripped in his hand.
'You haven't heard it all,
my dear girl,' he said,
wiping the tears from my eyes.
'A man takes his member
(I know you saw Richard's
when you were both smaller
and took baths together);
and it grows big and hard
like the bull's,
he places it
right here in his woman.'
With that I tore free.
I ran and I ran.
I hid in the cow shed.

I was never Small again
until Emily met you,
Mister Ira. Only to you
can I tell such horrible things.

Damn, my fingers have grown stiff
clutching this pen,
feel like dry twigs
itching to snap.
The breeze is warm though,
catches the branches.
Sometimes they float,
faery as ferns,
sometimes they droop
heavy as heartaches.
Get up, old girl,
the cliffs aren't far.
The islands in the straight
are dogs leaping into
the thick afternoon mist.
Go sit on those cliffs,
Emily. Your dreams
bits of cedar you toss
out to sea. Your dogs
catch them, carry them
west in their jowls,
drop them at the feet
of an invisible shore.
Sit on those cliffs,
let the sun wrap
you in the cedars'
warm shadows.
Sit on those cliffs,
feel everything recede.
Sexless, ageless,
you are Small again.

A Skidegate Pole

Entering the sheer
exuberance
of sky

the forest rears
into crests,

unleashes

them through the cedar boughs,
whirling each crown.

Before the delicate ache
between waves
collapses them,
one roaring into the other

      quiet

      falls,
      subtly—a seed

      of green
      light
      tumbling through darkness.
      Listen to it

      fall—

      its genesis
      endless

      while the forest seamlessly
      closes
      over like water.

The shaft
light carves falling
wears the many
faces
the wind chisels.

Under the blade of each
gust
the shaft gives in
to the soft
wooden features
of dark.

Inside me
the memory of first quiet
wells,
its message

hieratic,
rising through fathomless
rings.

As waves of light
stretch
one moment of growth
into the next,

the skin of my many faces
thickens to bark;

swaying
my quiet takes
roots.

WEST OF DARKNESS

The war is staggering. All has grown quiet,
bewildered in my heart. Even the darkness
skulks after dusk, wringing its hands, as the war
perfects itself. There is no time, ever,
to pause, to rethink. The wind rolls the ocean
onto its belly. Branches drum the tentative clearings.

But will second growth burst from the clearings?
Nothing responds except the quiet
the wind shakes free of the pent ocean.
We are nothing beside the darkness
of our unknowing. Though we persist ever
into night, few answers guide us. I am stupified by war.

At lunch Alice and I listened to the war
news from London: unaccountable dead in clearings
ripped through buildings by Hitler's bombs. Do monsters ever
know suffering? This evening the quiet
was jagged with a child's voice cutting the darkness.
The wind catches my bones, abrades the ocean.

What certainties are left us? I remember the ocean
as a child would, calm as a dog on a spring day. What is war
but tumult that has outlet. *Through the thick darkness*
Thy kingdom is hastening. Even in the dimmest clearings
the air rings with peace, with quiet,
though the nations of hell plot to expel Him forever and ever.

It will not be thus ever.
The profound earth and its attributes and the unquiet ocean
resist the wind, sink into the fecund quiet
of forest. *I cannot define my life, yet it is.* No war
can disturb the vigorous clearings
of the soul. God's voice flickers as we pass into darkness.

Somewhere there is a place west of darkness
I visit in dreams, a beach I wake from each time I ever
plan to remain. Beyond there are clearings
filled with illumined buildings. The ocean
washes them in late afternoon blue. There is no war.
Wind ribs sky with fingers of quiet.

By my fire's smoldering darkness, I am content in bed. The ocean
roars, ever fitful with this dreadful war.
From cloud clearings the moon knocks on my pane. Embers crackle
 their quiet.

QUIET

I have never ceased

to wonder at how trees

stand without thought

in their moment of growth

It is only I who divide

them by name

fit cedar arbutus alder

faun-soft branches dripping

with the final

light of the moon

The trees bend in one motion

each in itself

still and reaching

My eyes draw me in

With every step (each lighter

than any I have taken)

the forest thickens

year after year

the trees like angels

waiting each branch

a wing folding

back into night

A KISS FOR CANADA

So this is immortality—
tea cakes and roses in December.
Today I turned seventy and *Klee Wyck*,
after a long and difficult birth,
is spanking fresh from Oxford University Press.
A few weeks old and already
she can kick up a fuss.
Just look at the thicket of guests
gathered to pay her respect.
Swaddled in a crisp jacket of paper
she is handed all round the room,
leafed through and coddled.

The speeches have been delivered.
Wires from across Canada
are read aloud by my hostess.
Unopened letters wait in my lap.
I lose myself in the arbutus
framed by the window beside me.
Its branches shred the afternoon
into silky ribbons of light.
Graceful as sprites they pirouette
round the room, jostling elbows,
feyly dripping over tables of sweets.
Glancing up from steamy cups of tea,
my townsmen brighten each time
their eyes gently meet
with my gaze. Even Alice,
half blind and lost in her twilight,
picks up her napkin and waves.

Out of nowhere a great kindness
kneels down beside me,
softly kisses my cheek.
Looking up from an armful
of crimson carnations, I colour,
beam into Eye's radiant face.

CEDAR

Age hangs over me
like bones

of an arm
articulate

in its lack of flesh,
the tips

of its fingers
softened by feathers

of cedar
floating on the wind

like chimes.

LAST LETTER TO BABOO

When I have been laid out under granite
in the wind pulled from Ross Bay,
snug against Mother and Father,
Edith, Lizzie, and Richard,
bind into packs the photographs
that fell like cards into my hands.
Their caught faces will no longer need
to be read. Letters from Eye, from Lawren,
from you, unfolded my darkness
with care. Place them refolded
between dog-eared pages of Whitman.
Wild flowers Small secretly pressed
in her Bible years later crumbled.
I funnelled their dust into a vial to keep
with my oils. Slip it among the pearls
Milly seldom roped round her neck.
Even now I sense their brief lustre
each time I hold them next to my skin.
The gold cufflink Mayo freed
from his shirt sleeve and gave me
so long ago still longs for its mate.
Wrap it with the leads and collars
of dogs that would dance at my feet,
impatient the moment I paused
during one of our splendid walks down the beach.
How I loved the last washes of sun
pouring over the mountains into the Strait.
Those colours call to me.
I hear my dogs bark.
When you find this pen and my brushes
they may still be wet.
Dry them in all in soft moss.

Dear Baboo, these are my totems,
my emblems of kinship.
When I have cut myself free of all longing,
pack them up in a box.
Bury it deep in the forest,
as the Indians would, in an unmarked grave.

The Clearing

Geese christen the sky.
Their calls
snag the quiet

hanging

like a net

over the forest,
light caught in their skeins
a stream

deepened by
time.
        Its current
now darkness
draws

strength
from my eyes.

Locked in its ebb

I settle,
declare myself

centre.
Yet I cannot say

this solace of trees

rippling in circles
around me

has left me unscarred.
I am tired.

Circles widen.

The land is not empty.

AT SAINT MARY'S PRIORY

Death comes like the sea,
suddenly.
             I have waited so long.

How long had I walked
one with its salt
breath, insensible of the land's abrupt
change into cliffs?
                 How long had I stood there gazing
absently,
compelled by its swell?
                 When will I be
enveloped utterly
in the transfiguring arms of my God?

My hair has been bound in linen.
The cloth is damp.
                 Its weight,
limp,
burns into my thoughts.
I feel chill fingers
search my wrists.
                 They constantly harrow
the furrows
that pleat my brow.
Dozing in my mouth, my tongue
is still.
                 Fanned by the slightest ebb
of my breath,
my lips are aflame with brine.

The Sister, a statue at the foot of my bed,
is bent
reading the breviary open in her
hands.
       Her lips are frozen
in a rapture of faith.
In the midst of life we are in death.
The slow release of the flesh

    March 2, 1945

AFTERWORD

I find that raising my eyes slightly above what I am regarding so that the thing is a little out of focus seems to bring the spiritual into clearer vision.

Avoid outrageousness and monstrosity. Be vital, intense, sincere. Distort if necessary to carry your point but not for the sake of being outlandish. Seek ever to lift the painting above the paint.' Emily wrote this statement of aesthetic intent in her journal during the early thirties. If I remember correctly, I stumbled upon it sitting, as writers are perversely wont to do, in a café one rainy afternoon somewhere along Victoria's Johnson Street. Her thoughts enchanted me; I found myself referring back to them again and again. They formed the basis of my approach to the writing of what I now see as a portrait. The woman who sat for me demanded a style that fit her. What emerged is representational rather than purely documentary, impressionistic rather than exact. She despised art that betrayed nothing of the artist.

Now the likeness is complete. The rapport I struck with Emily or rather Emily struck with me has matured me. By example, as a writer and painter Emily has shown me that art matters only if what is rendered is true to the spirit of the subject. Without that spirit no precision in detail, no flourish in technique is worthy of attention and should be viewed with suspicion. The Emily I present is not unlike the actual woman whose life coincided with the first seventy-odd years of British Columbia's history within Canada. Yet the two ladies do have their differences. 'You should not have said that,' one Emily could censure the other. What do these differences mean?

My task to uncover the real Emily would have been a great deal more frustrating had two very important books not been published soon after I began work on *West of Darkness*. Maria Tippett's paradigmatic and loving *Emily Carr* and Doris Shadbolt's *The Art of Emily Carr*, with its generous number of colour plates, have been invaluable. I feel a great debt to both writers. I also owe much to Robin Skelton, who made me realize 'the importance of being Emily' and who has watched over the six-year gestation of this book with the benevolence of a god, cajoling me to press on when I needed rallying, cautioning me one or two years ago to finish by a certain All Hallows; it passed, but, like all gods, Robin had an interest in Emily's soul.

I also thank my mother, Nancy Barton, who seeded in me early on an interest in Emily. When I was Small's age I needed to compile a scrapbook on great Canadians to fulfil a requirement of my Blue Star for Wolf Cubs—I was a member of the 31st Beavers in Calgary. My mother provided magazine clippings about Emily (and others) and helped me with the wording (I still have the scrapbook on file):

> Emily Carr was a painter and writer who was born in 1871 in Victoria, B.C. where she lived most of her life. She died there in 1945. Her home was the 'House of all Sorts.' She kept lots of animals, especially cats which she loved. She painted many Indians who were her friends and loved her and called her 'Klee Wyck'—the laughing one.

How my ten-year-old self determined that Emily raised cats I have no idea! At any rate, Emily took her place in my imagination beside Lester Pearson, Pauline Johnson, Colonel James McLeod, LaSalle, Sir Wilfred Grenville, the Masseys, the Vaniers, and Stephen Leacock (who was my godfather's uncle). More important was the enthusiasm and pride my mother shared with me for what I now see as a focus left to us all by history. Years later, when I moved to Victoria in my early twenties, Emily's life was one of the few local legends familiar to me. I gravitated to her.

As I compiled this book I began to question the legend itself, wanting to correct what I perceived to be distortions, realizing Emily contributed largely to its creation. Therefore, whose version of her life should I accept? I found myself wondering. Hers, which skirts many issues? Or her biographers', which perhaps betray too many of her secrets? In the end I absorbed something of all points of view, but what I have come up with is only another version. I believe it is faithful to the woman herself, the one who is at the heart of her. I know I have composed out of respect.

So much for aesthetics. I am tempted to say what finally gets written simply is. Yet I find I am always asking myself questions, the kind I must have considered while writing *West of Darkness*. They all revolve around a central theme. What is that? you ask. You tell me. *Whose voice is speaking? What is the first person singular anyway? Who is this woman? What links us? How can I see her or any other life with any hope of clarity? How can people really know each other? Who am I?*

Victoria
July 1984

My Emily Carr

Every existence has its idiom.

—Walt Whitman

It is now twelve years since the publication of the first edition of *West of Darkness*, fifteen years since I completed the final manuscript, and twenty-one years since the first poem was written. Right from the very beginning, I knew I had found a subject that would preoccupy me so completely I could write a book-length work. Emily became my muse and my anchor for six years, and she captivates me still. Last winter, as I prepared this new edition for publication, I heard the poems I wrote all those years ago continue to speak to me with conviction, and it was Emily's voice that I heard speak them. I have maintained an on-going relationship with her built upon years of familiarity and association. I keep up with Carriana as best I can by reading the biographies and studies published about her since this book first appeared in 1987, and by attending exhibitions of her work. I have managed to view almost every major canvas and drawing, though there are a few I have yet (but hope someday) to see.

Over the last twelve years I have had a lot of time to think about my motives for writing what in Canada would be called a documentary poem about Emily Carr. I have also considered how those motives have been, or could be, interpreted in light of certain assumptions that have shaped recent aesthetics.

Just after *West of Darkness* was published in 1987, the rhetoric of cultural appropriation was being voiced for the first time in mainstream literary circles. It was not, however, in the air—or at least in the air that I knowingly breathed—during the years I wrote about Emily. Her legacy became a convenient target for criticism because she had found inspiration for art in the totems and villages of the Pacific Northwest's First Nations (a term she would not have been familiar with). Though I was never openly accused of any error in judgement for choosing to write about her relationship with native culture, I started to anticipate slights and became increasingly sensitive to—and even paranoid about—any suggestion that I may have consciously (or worse, unconsciously) annexed experience more in the purview of native poets. Foolishly castigating myself for being indifferent to, or ignorant of, their "prior claim" to my intuitively chosen subject material, I feared accusations that I had stolen and likely misinformed a readership more deservedly theirs.

For the faint of heart, writing in Canada became, and even today is, an ill-advised art of second guessing. I know better now, for as a gay writer I have learned that no matter how I choose to couch my material in anticipation of my audience, someone, straight or gay, will always take offence. Such reactions are part of my message.

Cultural appropriation, of course, does have its shadowy antecedents. While I was writing my first Emily Carr poems in Victoria in the late 1970s, a friend questioned why I wanted to write what she called "white Indian poetry," which in her opinion seemed to be unfortunately fashionable at the time, and, looking back, was being written to good affect by such poets as Sean Virgo and Susan Musgrave, among others. "White Indian poets" were accused of commandeering as their own the shamanistic space of native tradition rather than accepting the challenge of exploring the spiritual concerns of their own time through the frame of their own culture. In my own defense I felt that "white Indian aesthetics" were not in sympathy with what I was trying to accomplish, so I resisted the label. Instead I was attempting to theorize the creative nexus of a white female artist preoccupied with what she feared to be the decline of the original inhabitants of her own country. She was aware and critical of the destructive influence of white society on native culture, and saw her desire to paint the abandoned villages and totem poles *in situ* as one way to create a record of their threatened presence. To ignore the native themes in Emily's work would have been to misrepresent her. There is no question native poets would write completely different poems about Carr and her native-inspired work. In fact, it would be very interesting to read such poems. However harshly critical these poets might or might not be of her take on their culture, I hope they would also realise how joyfully she would celebrate their strong voices more than five decades after her death.

To understand what actually motivated me to write *West of Darkness*, it is perhaps more useful to connect it with Margaret Atwood's *The Journals of Susannah Moodie*, which inspired me enormously. Where Atwood's protagonist is "bushed" by the uncompromising Ontario wilderness of the early to mid-1800s, mine views the natural world of the Pacific Northwest as a sentient, benevolent force that is the incarnate expression of her God. Wrongly or rightly, I wrote *West of Darkness* as a refutation of Atwood's Susannah Moodie to show a different kind of survival (to repeat that now bankrupt Canadian literary cliché). Instead of "Your place is empty," I wrote "The land is not empty."

Feminism was also omnipresent while I was writing *West of Darkness*, and I was very aware that I was a man writing in a woman's voice. I took as my model the narrator of Sinclair Ross's *As For Me and My House*, whose voice, in my opinion, is believably a woman's from the first sentence on. At the time I would have been more than satisfied if I were able to approximate a similarly accomplished level of mimicry. I was also aware how closely Emily's life followed the paradigm of the woman artist who is challenged by patriarchy, so I attempted as much as possible to work that theme into the poems. Once, at some literary event soon after the book was published, a female academic asked me if it were suitable for me, as a man, to appropriate the voice of a female artist. Hers seemed to me to be an easy question inspired less by curiosity than intellectual fashion. I pointed out that Emily Carr left more than ample record of her own voice through her writings and that my challenge had been to equal that voice, and perhaps, through a facsimile of that voice, to re-voice certain things Emily consciously and unconsciously distorted in her reminiscences. Even now I see what I have written in Emily's voice as existing alongside of and subordinate to, rather than in place of, what Emily wrote.

More recently I was asked by another writer why I would want to write poetry in the voice of an artist rather than draft a critical essay about that artist's work, implying I had made a strange aesthetic decision. At the time I had no real answer beyond that it had not occurred to me to do otherwise. Upon reflection, however, I concluded that art criticism and poetry have entirely different aims: the former to stand outside and evaluate and the latter to stand inside and experience. *West of Darkness* was never intended to be a work of art history. Perhaps the question was posed out of an unexpressed belief that my creative motivation to write about Carr was parasitic. I could contend that all art is parasitic, for much inspiration is based upon vicarious, if symbiotic observation. I could also contend that good art only emerges out of how well we use our medium (language, paint) to mediate and explore our vicarious understandings. My decision to adopt a persona to make art was simply more obvious among the many aesthetic choices that writers make to address their material. Perhaps this question also unwittingly exposes latter-day fallout from the cultural appropriation debate. To write criticism rather than creative work is the stealth technology a writer might deploy to deflect anti-appropriationist attacks without anyone noticing.

I have made almost no revisions to the second edition. Most significantly, I have recast the subtitle of *West of Darkness* as "Emily Carr, a self-portrait" rather than the former "A portrait of Emily Carr," a change provoked by an early review that appeared in The British Columbia Library Association *Reporter*. The reviewer, who was (and may still be) the librarian at the Vancouver Art Gallery, questioned why "if this is Emily speaking, why is the subtitle 'Portrait' and not 'Self-Portrait?'" Her remark has haunted me for years, so I welcome the opportunity to address it.

The only other alterations involve the correction of a few typographical errors and of one minor, but embarrassing grammar mistake, one single-word substitution, one single-word insertion, the re-titling of one poem, and the addition of "Swirl," a poem dropped from the final manuscript of the first edition. The fifty-eight poems collected here hold up very well, so I was not tempted to rewrite them. I have never felt it appropriate when poets extensively revise their earlier work prior to republication. It seems to me to be an insult to the poets they once were. If the poems are embarrassing, suppress them.

I would like to thank Joy Gugeler and her staff at Beach Holme for keeping *West of Darkness* in print and thereby keeping my Emily Carr alive. I would also like to thank the many people who have supported me and my Carr project, especially the late Robin Skelton, my famly, Lala Heine Koehn, Neile Graham, James Gurley, Kathryn McLeod, Alison Beaumont, John Flood (the publisher of the original edition), Blaine Marchand, Barry Dempster, Kristjana Gunnars, Kate Braid, Rita Donovan and Helen Humphreys, who have all said such nice things to me about *West of Darkness* over the years.

Neena Singhal also merits thanks for her transcription into electronic form of a book written prior to the stand-alone PC. We all write in solitude, hoping to be read and read well. It is a feeling I am sure Emily, who knew isolation perhaps better than any other Canadian artist, would have wholeheartedly identified with.

In the years since *West of Darkness* was published I have come to wonder how Emily would perceive me. Would she consider me to be an appropriate (auto)biographer? Would she consider me a good person? How would she judge me for being gay? Would she have called me a 'bugger,' or used some similar label to describe me? Would she question my right to tell her story? Such considerations never occurred to me while I was writing about her. The voice I heard speaking through me while writing these poems was warm, benevolent and searching, and not in any way judgmental. Nor did I define myself as gay at the time. Consequently, it is only in the last ten years that I have come to see Emily as my drag persona. (*How she would hate that!*). Given that most drag artistes lip-synch retro disco hits or show tunes, my choice of drag identity is perhaps iconoclastic. In any case, my twenty-one-year connection to her through this book may be the cause of my anxieties about her good (or bad) opinion of me. Or are these anxieties the self-conscious frailties of a Dorian Gray uncertain what his portrait betrays about his soul? Who is *West of Darkness* the portrait of anyway? Its subject or its author? Perhaps both. We all hope that those we love will favour us with returned affection, that they will see something of themselves in how we see them.

Ottawa
July 1999

Acknowledgements

The author would like to thank the following magazines where some of the poems originally appeared, sometimes in slightly different forms, on occasion under different titles.

ARC: *Clearing, Guyasdams' D'Sonoqua, Queen Charlotte Islands Totem*; ARIEL: *Red Cedar, Strait of Juan de Fuca*; THE CANADIAN FORUM: *Cedar*; CANADIAN LITERATURE: *Grey*; THE DALHOUSIE REVIEW: Story Draft; DANDELION: Invocation; DESCANT: *A Skidegate Pole, Laughing Forest*; THE DINASAUR REVIEW: Metchosin Sketching Trip, Goldstream Flats, Lizzie's Death; FIDDLEHEAD: Portents; FOLEY TRAIL: *Quiet*; GRAIN: Mother Was Gentle; ISLAND: *Autumn In France*; LOS: Saturday Evening (A Letter To Lawren Harris); THE MALAHAT REVIEW: *Woo, Indian Church, Big Raven, Nirvana, Blunden Harbour, Sunshine and Tumult, Above The Trees*, Haro Strait, East Anglia Sanitorium, 1903: A Recurring Dream, *Swirl**, *Quiet*; NEBULA: Return To The East, The Totems Permit Me Peace, *Edge Of The Forest*, Boxing Day, 1934, West of Darkness, At Saint Mary's Priory; THE NEWEST REVIEW: *Forsaken, Scorned As Timber, Beloved Of The Sky, Masset Bears*; NORTHERN LIGHT: Small's Cow Song, Full Moon; NORTHWARD JOURNAL: Life Class, Last Letter To Baboo, Monday Morning, Sophie Frank; OUTPOSTS (Great Britain): 316 Beckley Street, Saint Joseph's Hospital, 1937; PRISM INTERNATIONAL: Two Sketches of San Francisco; QUARRY: *Vanquished, Laughing Bear*; QUEEN'S QUARTERLY: *Forest, British Columbia, Old Tree at Dusk, Tree, Wood Interior, Above The Gravel Pit*; UNIVERSITY OF WINDSOR REVIEW: *Jack-In-The-Pulpit* Remembered.

* 'Swirl' did not appear in the first edition.

The author wishes to acknowledge the assistance of the Canada Council for the Arts in the writing of the first edition of this book.

The quotes heading each section are taken from *Hundreds And Thousands: The Journals of Emily Carr* (Clark, Irwin & Company Limited, Toronto / Vancouver, 1966). 'Inspiration is intention obeyed,' at the beginning of section three, Emily quotes from an unidentified source. The quotes in "West of Darkness" are from different poems in Walt Whitman's *Leaves of Grass*.

'Mothering Sunday'** and 'Mother Was Gentle' are dedicated to Alison Beaumont, 'Story Draft' to Neile Graham, 'Life Class,' in all its parts, to Kathryn McLeod.

** 'Mothering Sunday' was published as 'Mother's Day' in the first edition.

John Barton is the author of seven award-winning collections of poetry including *Notes Toward a Family Tree* (co-winner of the 1995 Ottawa-Carleton Book Award), *Designs from the Interior* (winner of the 1995 Archibald Lampman Award) and *Sweet Ellipsis* (winner of the 1999 Archibald Lampman Award). The first edition of *West of Darkness* won the Archibald Lampman Award in 1988. He is the co-editor of *Arc: Canada's National Poetry Magazine* and has been published in literary magazines in Canada, Australia, the U.S. and the U.K. He lives in Ottawa.